A Battleaxe and a Metal Arm 16:

The Slumbering Bog

Samuel Fleming

Cover Art by David Leahey

ISBN-13: 978-1-954679-48-1 (paperback)
ISBN-13: 978-1-954679-47-4 (ebook)

Thank you to my Beta Readers

And, as always, to my First Reader,

Mel.

Contents

"I can say for certain that the most painful death is the one that extinguishes hope. After that they are rather painless."
—wavering

Previously...

Helesys, Taunauk, and Shawn had journeyed far since their first tentative steps through the dungeon. In the realm of the fishmen, they learned that they would be reborn and that they could bring back treasures. In the barracks, Zhug gifted them the Everfall shield, and the giant told them just how rare their power was but that even the Chosen needed to fear the lingering deaths that plagued the realms. In the Wode, they met trapped demigods and saw the first evidence of the Gatekeeper. They would first taste of the limits of the realms, but both Helesys and Taunauk would ultimately perish before climbing the infinite wall. Nor would they find solace past the underground tunnels or the buried hive.

In the realm of the wizard's tower, they first met Shawn, and found the Ring of Winter. At the end of a perilous climb, they met the wizard Amadeus and learned the horrible truth about the dungeon—that it was a soul trap of unimaginable power and size. Then they came face-to-face with the Wolf King for the first time, as the God of the dungeon possessed their ally and turned Amadeus against them.

They woke in a misty jungle without Shawn, and in the depths of the Apothecary's lair, Helesys learned how to pry apart the seams and walk between worlds without death. They found Shawn in the next realm, on an endless beach. They sailed aboard the ill-fated ship, the Malorienta, and find a second iteration of Pitiful Lull, a creature shattered and spread across the realms. They perished at the ends of the ocean and woke alone on a beach. The mysterious Voice at Meridian addressed Helesys by name and admitted to giving them the power to bring artefacts back after death. The Voice sought the defeat of the Wolf King, and pointed them toward The Machine of Antrikaumora that lay at the bottom of the endless sea.

Helesys and Taunauk woke and journeyed through the City of Shéslang, desperately avoiding the parasite, the Duoausongur. With the Jade Lemur they flew high and met with the withered God Serpent, itself. It offered knowledge that three brothers who once sought to defeat the Wolf King had failed. With the magic spear, they found Shawn in the realm of the Cogheart. They bested the renegade warrior Dissimul and spoke with the machine god, One-Mind, who repaired a connection in Helesys's metal arm—one that was severed before she was imprisoned.

Their travel to the Godpeak was intercepted, and the heroes were trapped in an alien ship. Helesys was able to break free of the Idnauthi control, and comb through their history logs. It was there that she saw the true form of the Dungeon for the first time—a bulbous, writhing cloud that moved as if it were alive, and could travel through space and time. Moments later, they fled the ship with freed Terrans in tow, and Helesys triggered the ship's launch sequence, hurtling them into space.

They fled into the castle's attic, a place packed with bodies of the lingering dead. The alien, Sigun, attacked them one last time, before succumbing to the blank-faced Terrans that infested the attic. Down the heroes crawled, through twisting catwalks and strange water landscapes, to fight clones of themselves at the bottom. At the end of the realm, they found a twisted forest of blood, glass, and metal, ruled over by Mr. Mask. Helesys bolstered the captive voices, freeing the many, and as the realm collapsed, they fled to the next realm.

In a frozen, wind-torn realm, they found the Godpeak. The heroes parted ways with the Idnauthi survivors before climbing the mountain. They survived terrible monsters and the cursed Wendigos, but in the end, a giant owl-guardian of the forest saved them and took them to the summit. It was there that Shawn learned that he was neither elven nor human—he was a wisp from the plane of dreams; one that took a mortal life. Taunauk found several spirits, including his father Rehkoros. He revealed that the Dungeon had appeared in Accaelum, the Endroggen afterlife, and trapped ten thousand souls. Taunauk had been the chosen champion and vessel to bring them home. Meanwhile, Helesys was plagued with partial visions of her mother and sister, but nothing so certain as her allies' visions. In the end, Shawn left them.

Helesys and Taunauk returned to Zhug's realm, and he lent them the diving crab, and they used it to dive beneath the endless sea. They made it to the dark ruins of Antrikaumora and fought through a kraken and mutated eels. In their journey, Helesys expressed desire to learn Endroggen rage, Taunauk agreed to teach her. In an underground, underwater vault, the heroes descended, and found the Machine of Antrikaumora hidden in the strange architecture built by a mysterious Terran named Sinatin Koh—whom they think to be the Voice at Meridian. And they discovered the truth—the Machine of Antrikaumora was an antimagic generator.

They stepped through the seam to a desert realm and found Shawn. He had met with the Voice at Meridian again, and it told him, only a god can kill another god—it would have to be Shawn that dealt the death blow to the Wolf King when the time came. Together, the three heroes walked to the city of Civirrea. It was there they were celebrated as Chosen ones and given respite, for a time. They learned that the Gatekeeper might be held hostage by the Wolf King. After, they fought in the pits, before being taken below the city to meet the Angel. They learned the history of Civirrea and saw the horrid etchings THE CHOSEN ARE A LIE. In the end, the Angel attacked them, saying that it was loyal to the Wolf King—the never risen sun. One of Taunauk's ancestors was permanently destroyed, but the heroes escaped.

Helesys, Taunauk, and Shawn appeared in the upper halls of the castle, and it was not long before they saw signs of the Wolf King. They found a bedroom, complete with trinkets, baubles, and paintings—all untouched for a long time. They pressed on, and found more paintings suddenly appearing in the hall.

Taunauk stepped through the first painting, and Helesys and Shawn tentatively followed. They emerged on the fields of Endroggen—a memory long since passed. Taunauk's home.

Moments later, Taunauk's father, Rehkoros, stood before them, and the three heroes stood as children. Taunauk wanted to see his mother, but the memory of Rehkoros—the illusion—stood its ground. In anger, Taunauk fought his father, while Helesys and Shawn fought other Endroggen, or what seemed to be Endroggen.

They felled the Endroggen, then retreated into the village. In a small tent, Taunauk again appeared as a boy and spoke with his young shield brother, Thuldreth. Thuldreth was in love with a girl, and this pained the young Taunauk, for it was something he could not have—not as Aonar. Not as the Vessel of his people. But in those bitter moments, Taunauk found resolve.

Next, they found a painting of the mountains of Eluthiya, the gate of the realm of dreams. Shawn bid them follow and to fly with him. In the end, only Helesys followed, for Taunauk was bound to his people. Helesys and Shawn surfed dreams, but were separated.

Helesys found herself on a hill overlooking a factory. And on that hill, she met the creature, Nimicus, mortal enemy of the wisps and the realm of dreams. Nimicus was not bound to the dungeon, and it came and went as freely as a dream. Shawn confessed that it had been the death of Tamir, the god of dreams, and in its death throes, the god had cut itself into a thousand wisps so that they might flee and live a while longer.

They walked the cobblestone path of a village and came to Shawn's mortal home. A grandfather and granddaughter welcomed him. To be a wisp was intoxicating, but to be mortal was so much more real than living a dream could ever be.

Helesys and Shawn returned to Taunauk and to the castle hall. There, she found her own painting, her own childhood. Her sister Aradi teased her for working so hard, while young Helesys lamented being the head of the family. Helesys's young life was one of tutors and hard work, Aradi's one of truancy and giftedness. In another memory, Helesys told her mother about her plans to join the elven legion, one that wore on Wynbella. Helesys learned of the sudden death of her father, and the reason her mother was hesitant for her to join the legion.

Next they saw the Eternal War, Bellum Aeternum, the struggle of the elves against the shadowkind writ large. Helesys flashed to memories of battle school, then to the fated day on the steppes overlooking the Passage of Sanhara. Helesys tried to push forward, but they were overwhelmed and Helesys's world went black.

She woke to a blinding light in a hospital room. Her right arm was missing, replaced by a metal one. Memories passed in a blur: Aradi visited her in the hospital, her mother didn't. Helesys relearned how to walk. Then another memory of her searching out the dungeon with Taunauk. They were looking for Shawn, right before they were trapped.

Helesys learned the terrible truth about that day on the Eternal Battlefield. She died, killed by a blast shell. Her arm torn off, her brain damaged. The wand-arm fitted and wired into her, to give her a second chance.

Helesys learned that she was a made-thing.

And in the aftermath, the heroes were thrust onto a stage to face the masters of the realm—mages and warriors congealed into wolves, aided by a giant of metal and a creature of shadow. The battle was vicious, and in the end, the comrades were victorious. Each had passed their test.

Now they walk the King's path, the same realms as the Wolf King. And at the end, they will find the God of the dungeon.

~ ~ ~

No Rest for the Chosen

Helesys tore open the seam upon the stage—sparing no time to contemplate the freshly fallen bodies of the nine. Whether they would disintegrate and reform in some other realm, or that they were beholden to the realm of paintings, Helesys didn't know. Helesys didn't care.

They had further to go, and she would not be denied escape. They had come too far. Seen too much.

The barren stage faded behind her as the heroes stepped through the seam and into the next world.

Now, *they walked the King's path,* or so the nine had said. Helesys wasn't sure what it meant, but if it was the way forward, then she wouldn't hesitate.

Helesys, Taunauk, and Shawn emerged from the seam and into a mist-covered swamp. The ground was spongy and covered in a dense moss, with little underbrush to speak of. The only other plants were ghost-white trees that wove together into a bramble canopy. Lichen hung like tattered curtains. The air was cool and though there was no breeze; the mist drifted through the swamp.

Suddenly, Helesys felt the next seam, like a splinter in her mind—the mist was drifting toward it.

She told this aloud to her companions, leaning on her spear, and pointing into the distance. "We need only follow the mist."

Shawn ran a hand under his hood, over his thin hair. The rogue's arms were bound tightly in black wrappings to seal his otherworldly powers. "Sure, into the spooky bog we go. Lovely. Lead the—"

The rogue trailed off as Taunauk pushed past, mountain of a man as sure-footed as a jungle cat. His hair and beard shaved short, cropped for battle. He already had his Everfall shield and his axe drawn, and he stalked forward, leading them.

Shawn met Helesys's eyes with a hint of concern. She took his meaning: The last realms had been hard on all of them. Each of the three had learned revelations about their lives and about their entrapment in the dungeon. And they hadn't yet had time to process these things.

Most recent of all, Helesys's own revelation. The metal fingers of her gauntlet twitched idly, as real to her as her own flesh and blood—there was no telling where she ended and the components began… even her mind—

Helesys grit her teeth, and merely said, "We'll talk later."

"Yeah," Shawn replied reluctantly.

Helesys followed Taunauk, and Shawn followed behind her. Together, the three pressed forward, following the drifting mist deeper into the swamp.

~

They crept through the swamp. Waiting. Listening for any signs of enemies or even life. Minutes stretched to hours, and there was not another living soul, save for the twisted trees and half-dead moss beneath their feet.

Silence was agony. Helesys didn't even have the ever-present voice of her wand any longer. Since her revelation in the last realm, the voice was gone.

Not gone—melded with Helesys's own self. Like so many other things, the separation of her and her wand was an illusion, like Helesys's white hair. Cropped short, and under illusion to look long.

In prior realms, to find the seam, the wand would guide her by subtle feeling or by voice. Now, Helesys merely *knew* where the seam was. In prior realms, she would have talked with her wand to gain insights into the past or to her own memories. Now memories came to her… well, like memories ought to. It felt as if little was withheld from her now. However, a few memories were obscured by the dungeon or locked away in her own mind.

Helesys thought of her mother, Wynbella. The two of them sitting on the edge of the bed while Wynbella brushed Helesys's hair. Mother liked her hair long. And then wandering the courtyard with her when her mother felt well enough to go outside.

Happy memories—a blanket in the fog.

"Something's out there," Taunauk whispered. "Can you see it?"

Helesys's attention came back to her surroundings. She couldn't *physically* see anything through the fog, so she extended her magical perception. There was something out there; she could feel it in her magical perception, like ripples in a pond. But whatever it was seemed to be all around, and not moving.

The moment dragged on, until Taunauk bashed his axe and shield together—a thud of metal and ironwood echoed through the swamp. "Come on!" he shouted. "Come out and fight!"

Only mist answered. Nothing moved, not even in Helesys's magical perception.

"Anything?" Shawn whispered, twin daggers drawn.

Helesys shook her head. "Nothing. Yet."

Taunauk growled, and his hand squeezed the leather wrap of his axe. Frustration oozed from him.

"Don't worry, big guy," Shawn said. "I'm sure we'll have plenty to fight before the realm is through."

Taunauk didn't reply. He merely started walking forward into the gloom. Helesys felt for him; of all the recent revelations they had, Taunauk's might've been the hardest: To have been raised to be a champion of his people, yet denied the life of an Endroggen. All so he could be a vessel for the souls imprisoned in the dungeon.

Taunauk had found his father, saved his father's soul. Yet the barbarian now seemed even more conflicted than ever.

Since the enemies hiding in the bog hadn't attacked yet, Helesys asked, "Have you spoken more with your father?"

"We had words," Taunauk replied quietly. Helesys wondered if he was worried about enemies or spirits overhearing him. "Some of worth, some…" He sighed and looked up, as if asking the heaven's for guidance. Finally, he said, "It is not an easy thing to mend the past."

"No," Helesys replied. "I don't suspect it is."

Shawn said, "It's a noble sentiment, but sometimes the past is lost to us. Sometimes it isn't worth it."

Helesys said, "It might not be worth it, but it's not lost."

"Sorry," Shawn said, "but Taunauk is a special case. He carries the past around with him."

Helesys replied, "That may be, but it does not matter. Even for you or I, we can come to terms with the past. Even if we can't change it."

Taunauk muttered, "Wise words."

Shawn stared off into the gloom and nodded along, either looking for danger or unable to meet her eyes. "Maybe you're right… Maybe it's different for those things still within our grasp. Other things feel impossibly far away. Lifetimes away."

The barbarian paused and looked back over his shoulder. "What is one lifetime, or two or three, compared to how far we've come? Nothing is beyond your grasp, Shawn, and surely not beyond the reach of Soldei Milent."

Shawn smirked. "For a man who speaks so little, you sure have some nuggets of wisdom."

"From a lifetime of listening, and not speaking incessantly." Taunauk returned the rogue's smirk.

Shawn replied, "You can go back to being the strong, silent type."

~

Soon, the ground beneath their feet grew damp, and then laden with water. Step by step they sank deeper into the swamp, the muck squelching beneath their boots, each step releasing a sour, earthen smell. For as unpleasant as the swamp looked, Helesys found it strange that they hadn't smelled much of anything until that point—only when the muck beneath their feet was disturbed.

A memory of a spell came to her, unbidden. "*Aqua deambu-latio*," she said. Slowly, the three heroes rose higher in the swamp until they were standing on top of the twisted grasses. Both Taunauk and Shawn paused to watch their feet.

Shawn said, "Your spell recall is fabulous, really. But you couldn't have remembered that *before* my boots got wet?"

"Of course not," she said jokingly. "Besides, I can't just re-member all the spells I used to know. It seems like I need *something* to trigger my memory."

"I'm only half serious," the rogue added. "I appreciate you. So, how do you know so many spells? I admit, I don't remem-ber a lot of mages, but you know a lot, and you know spells from different schools of magic."

Helesys thought back to her revelation. She was an accom-plished mage, but she was also a made-thing, directly connected to her wand. She had years of knowledge and the innate magical abilities from the wand itself—something she still didn't fully understand.

In their time through the dungeon, Helesys, Taunauk, and Shawn had shared nearly everything with each other: All of their recaptured memories and all of their struggles. But Helesys felt uneasy at the thought of telling her companions that she had died on the battlefield, that she'd been brought back from death, and turned into something else.

A *made-thing*.

Instead, she told a half-truth. "It's my wand-arm. When they *fixed* me, they connected me to the wand. I know every-thing that it knows."

Taunauk asked, "Has the wand given you anymore in-sight?"

She shook her head, though Taunauk was marching in front of her and didn't see it. "My wand has been silent since the castle." Since the revelation. Since she realized that the wand's persona wasn't really there—

In a strange way, Helesys had been talking to herself.

Suddenly, magic flared through the swamp, crashing into Helesys like a wave. The muck and grass beneath their feet began to writhe. Ghost-white roots upended and undulated through the air, like the swamp itself was stirring from a fitful sleep.

All at once, the heroes readied, and roots reached out to them through the air. They met the assault with purple power and blades, scorching tendrils and lopping off others. With each blow struck, the roots grew more agitated, until they were lashing through the air like bullwhips.

For a moment, the heroes stumbled, none ready to call upon their otherworldly powers so early in the realm.

Helesys kindled power. While holding the *water walk* spell, she cast another, splitting her concentration. "*Amplificare potentia,*" she shouted. This time her touch upon their powers was light—careful to increase only their physical strength and speed, not Endroggen Rage or a Wisp's etherealness. It was a far smaller boon, but it would be enough.

Bolstered by Helesys, the three became a blur, meeting each lashing vine with their own attack. In moments, they were beating back the oppressive swamp, leaving piles of severed vine and root at their feet.

The battle was fierce and short-lived. The heroes stood victorious as roots slithered back into the muck and the swamp stilled.

"What did I say?" Shawn asked, holstering his daggers. "Did I say something offensive?"

Helesys felt the magic subside. Again, she was struck with the sensation of a slumbering giant drifting back to sleep.

"It's us, I think," Helesys said. "This wouldn't be the first realm that took notice of our presence."

Shawn shifted uneasily. "You say that like this place is alive."

Taunauk grunted, giving Helesys a sidelong glance, but didn't chastise her for the spell. "We've seen stranger things."

Shawn replied, "Can't we have one normal-ish realm?"

Taunauk sighed. "Don't give breath to fate." Both he and Helesys shot the rogue a look.

Shawn held up his hands. "Alright, alright. I walk in silence."

The heroes returned to their journey, pressing deeper into the swamp, even more on edge than before. But Helesys drifted back to the battle and to battles past. Many times she'd split her power, concentrating on two or even three spells at a time. She hadn't seen other mages split their power as she had.

Helesys looked again to her wand-arm, wondering what other gifts she'd been unknowingly given.

~

Hours dragged on in the swamp, and Helesys's gauntlet grew to a dull heat from holding the water walk spell. She'd grown stronger since One-Mind had fixed the connection in her wand-arm, but it felt as if she'd been made for bursts of power instead of drawn out spells.

She paused at the thought: She *had* been made.

She had been a soldier in the elven legion, and her surgery wouldn't have been an accident. The wand would've been specially chosen, the metal of her arm specially forged. Helesys had been one of the best soldiers in the legion. Now she was a living weapon.

So, why, in the name of Novissimé, had she been allowed to leave? Why would the legion part with their greatest weapon?

The question wracked her mind as they walked through the fog.

Her mother had tried to convince her to stay…

Aradi, her sister, had told Helesys about the dungeon. Helesys had sought out the dungeon. For what? In hopes that it would save her shattered mind? Her broken body?

It didn't make sense. But she must have had a reason for seeking out the dungeon. Helesys *felt* she had a reason. Misguided as it might've been.

She must have been desperate when she woke from the surgery. She wasn't herself. Wasn't thinking clearly.

A pit formed in Helesys's stomach as they walked. She had been a wreck when she woke from surgery. She remembered. Half-alive, half-dead.

Even now, so far removed from that fateful day, Helesys could still feel the tumultuous emotions that swirled in her. She really had been nothing but pain and rage and fear. Like she'd been shattered into a thousand pieces and only the most jagged piece of her had been left.

~ ~ ~

Witchbane Ruins

Twice more, Helesys felt the swamp stirring with magic, but neither time did roots lash out at them. Instead, the muck beneath their feet rolled like dying waves. Both times, it passed quickly and without fanfare.

After the second time, Shawn asked, "What do you think that means?"

"Does it matter?" Helesys asked earnestly.

Shawn's face wrinkled in a frown. "Maybe not… but if this place is really alive, I would rather the place be consistent and dumb. Not smart and biding its time."

Taunauk grumbled at the rogue's remark, but said nothing. Helesys was inclined to agree with both of them, with Shawn's worry and about the rogue giving voice to it.

Soon, the white trees grew denser, their towering branches even more twisted—until the canopy above them was a rolling mass of white bark. Strange cat-like creatures chased each other through the limbs, never coming close nor slowing for her to make out more than a vague shape. They were dappled green, and climbed with spider-like dexterity—spiraling playfully through the tangled limbs. The only sound was the scratching of their nails on the bark.

Smaller trees appeared. Once again, unease gripped the weaver, as Helesys saw the shape of them. Each smaller tree was Terran-shaped, with two arms and two legs—ghostly figures.

Shawn stepped close to one of them, eyeing the face hidden in the bark. "Creepy bastards. What do you suppose—"

The rogue jumped back. The tree twisted in a wide, slow arc, its bark groaning in protest. It lasted only a few moments before it stopped, like a single step of a terrible waltz. The last thing to move was a ripple of bark where the head of the thing might've been, like a face twisting in agony beneath a bedsheet.

After, a single white flower sprouted from the branch. Shawn took another step back.

"Alright," he said. "I'm good and creeped out now. How far away is the seam?"

From above came a quiet voice. "It's rude to refuse a gift."

A large green cat lay above them in the branches of the canopy. Its body was long and slender, nearly serpentine. Its fur was the color of dark leaves. The smaller cats were nowhere to be seen.

Without pause, Shawn replied, "A gift, you say? How do you know that?"

The green cat's tail twitched. "I've lived here longer than you've wandered, young one. I know many things about the slumbering bog." Its voice was soft as a purr.

Taunauk grunted, sparing only a glance at the cat before looking back across the swamp. "We've heard many such boasts, creature. Do you mean to help us or harm us? If it's the latter, get on with it."

Helesys watched the cat as it met her eyes curiously. She felt no warning from her wand-arm.

She asked, "Have you heard of the King's Path?"

"You mean the path you walk on? The path Chosen search for? The path the King himself once walked? Then, yes. I have. You are at the threshold of it, weaver. You are why the slumbering bog stirs. It knows why you're here. There isn't much time. You need to be quick. Journey through the bog before it wakes."

Shawn asked, "What happens then?"

The green cat leaned forward on wiry-muscled legs. "First you will sink, and the bog will eat you. Wring your bones dry. Your skin will harden, and eventually, you'll be tall enough for my children to play on your limbs."

The heroes' eyes drifted around the swamp, taking in the ghost-white trees with new regard.

Helesys sighed wearily. "It wouldn't be the first time a realm tried to take us." She thought of Mr. Mask's realm of blood and glass, and the gallery in the castle the realm before.

"Spoken like true Chosen," the big cat said. "What do you have to fear? You'll make it through the slumbering bog and through the King's path. You'll either survive or you will die."

Shawn said, "Alright, little kitty. Run along. The grownups have had enough. We're going into the creepy bog."

The green cat stood and stretched, its back arching high above—abnormally long. "Very well. Beware the witch hunters up ahead. They... Let's just say they've lost their sense. They know only the hunt." It stared down at Helesys. "And you look awfully like a witch to me." Then it turned and snaked up the branches.

Shawn said, "You know, if we never met another weird-shaped, cryptically speaking creature, it would be too soon."

~

Sometime later, they came upon ruins. Shattered tone blocks lay strewn across the marsh. Pillars lay half-embedded in the ground, vines creeping over them. Beyond were the remains of what might've been a cathedral or a palace. It rose five stories into the air, the bramble canopy parting to make room for it, as if afraid to touch the stones. No vines covered its surface, and the whole of it listed at an angle as if it were starting to sink into the muck. The bulk of the structure extended into the depths of the forest like some titanic corpse.

The heroes approached wearily. Helesys could sense lingering magic. It seemed to pour out of the ruins like a leaking siv, though the vine-covered columns and blocks felt cold and lifeless in comparison. Even so, they crept around the stones, relying on the *water walk* spell to keep them quietly atop the grasses.

Taunauk whispered, "Do you sense anything?"

Helesys told them of the lingering magic. "But I don't sense any life—"

Whoops and hollers carried through the bone-white trees. Terran-like excitement. There was little cover near the heroes, so they crouched beside one of the fallen pillars. Helesys cursed the waist-high cover.

A half dozen Terrans ran out of the darkness. They reminded Helesys of barbarians—clad in furs and animal skins, and carried an array of axes and curved swords. They entered the clearing and their cheers abruptly stopped when they saw Helesys, Taunauk, and Shawn.

"At least they're human," Shawn muttered.

Taunauk stood tall and called out, "We are passing through, and mean you no harm. We would have words."

The Terrans glanced at each other, confusion written on their faces. Two of the farthest began to walk closer, fanning out as they did.

One of the Terrans, who wore a bone-tooth necklace, stepped forward, hands out in supplication. "No harm here. Just hunting." His voice was hoarse, his eyes crazed.

Taunauk glanced at the ruins, and the hunter followed his gaze. The barbarian said, "There's magic here. Is it dangerous?"

The hunter shook his head. "Not for you… for her." He pointed to Helesys. The other hunters took careful steps, widening their group. Helesys kindled power in her wand-arm and tried not to let annoyance show on her face.

Shawn called out, "She's with us. If there's trouble for her, then there's trouble for *you*."

The hunters looked at Taunauk, and the barbarian nodded. Helesys wondered if they thought he was another one of their kind or their tribe, seeing as how Taunauk wore furs like they did.

The lead hunter scowled. "She reeks of magic. She's a witch!"

Taunauk replied, "The choice is yours: Words or steel?"

The hunters screamed and ran toward them—two straight for them, while those on the ends ran wide to flank.

Helesys raised her metal hand. "*Immotalem immortalis.*" Fire blossomed from her hand in a wide spray, showing the swamp in light. The two approaching hunters disappeared behind a wall of flames.

She turned and fired a volley of arcane blasts at the two hunters approaching from the center. One was blindsided and was sent tumbling backward over a fallen pillar. Taunauk met the other in a flash of magic steel. On the other side, Shawn met the other two hunters in a blur, and Helesys sensed magic from their enemies.

A scream came from behind her. Helesys turned back toward her side as her two hunters emerged from the fire, their furs smoldering and faces wild.

"*Greim oirre,*" Helesys said, extending her reach to all around. Vines leapt from the stones and lashed at the hunters—only one of Helesys's enemies were slowed. She met him with her spear and their weapons clashed. As she spun around, she saw that only two other foes were slowed by the vines— the plants slid off the other enemies as if they were coated in oil.

The weaver cursed under her breath and she turned back to her foe. Splitting her concentration between *water walk* and the *vines* should've given them an edge, but she felt sinister workings. The hunters were tainted with magic—as if they were warded creatures instead of men.

While one of her enemies struggled against the vines, Helesys stepped back. She feinted, letting her spear fall, letting the hunter think he had the upper hand. She churned power in her gauntlet. When he raised his sword to strike, she leveled her gauntlet at his torso.

The spreadblast cut him in half. Flesh and blood sprayed back, coating the entangled hunter in red. He screamed, face twisted in anger.

Another hunter fell by Taunauk's axe. Another by Shawn's dagger.

A shout came from the top of the ruins. "*Restu sonmova, venatores!*"

Helesys braced herself to counter the spell, but the three remaining hunters froze where they stood. Tentatively, she released her vines, and readied herself for the newcomer.

A cloaked figure walked out from the ruins. They were draped in bone jewelry. When they neared the heroes, they pulled back their hood. The woman's face was crisscrossed with scars and wrinkles.

She looked at the hunters, one at a time, then shook her head. "Forgive them. They don't know what they do." When the heroes didn't follow right away, she added, "You have nothing to fear from me, or from the ruins, but if you stay out here, more witch hunters will come for you."

It was Shawn who moved first, gesturing for them to follow. Together, they walked into the ruins.

~

"My name is Beliah," the woman said. Helesys, Taunauk, and Shawn followed behind her. The weaver had let go of the *water walk* spell.

The passageways they walked were wide and nearly worn smooth by decay. Not even the walls or the ceiling were spared—the designs were gone and only faint engraving lines remained.

Shawn gave their names, then asked, "What is this place?"

"Ruins of what used to be."

"Okay… but what did it *used to* be?"

Beliah turned and led them up several flights of stairs. "It used to be an outpost in the wilds. A respite at the edges of the known world. Now the bog is stirring and reclaiming this place."

Shawn's face wrinkled in confusion, and Helesys held up a hand to silence him.

Beliah led them to the top floor and to a large room. Unlike the rest of the ruins, the stones here were immaculate. Candlelight spilled over ornate carvings of strange beasts, casting long, flickering shadows. Scrap wood littered the floor. A small living quarters lay in a distant corner of the room—little more than a cot and open boxes of clothes and supplies. Arrow-slits lined the far wall.

Shawn said grimly, "This used to be an outpost?"

Beliah nodded. She waved her hand and muttered words. Rubbish and wood swirled on the floor, drifting across the room, and assembling into chairs for the four of them. They sat facing one another.

"There used to be more of us. Now I'm all that's left. This place used to be a dream." Beliah gestured to the flickering carvings on the walls. "But it's been pilfered and gutted. I can only stay the rancid magic of the bog for so long. A dream dismantled so we could survive a little longer."

Helesys glanced around, but saw no evidence of another soul. There was only one cot in the corner. "Apologies, but you keep saying *we*. There's no one else here."

"Out there." Beliah pointed. "The hunters are what's left of my people—don't worry, I hold no ill will for their loss. You defended yourselves, as you should."

Taunauk asked, "Why did they attack us?" Everfall leaned against his chair, his father's axe lay across his lap.

"They've lost themselves. The bog has hold of them, and has claimed them piece by piece."

Shawn leaned forward, elbows on his knees, and shook his head. "I don't get it. Why stay here? And why aren't you… crazy, like them?"

Beliah let out a deep sigh. "Forgive me. It's been some years since I've spoken to anyone at length, and some know more than others by the time they arrive. It is customary to start at the beginning. You are Chosen, are you not?"

"We are," Helesys replied. "We are on the King's path."

Beliah nodded. "Of course. Only Chosen wander here. It is said that the first Chosen built these halls on their way to challenge the Wolf King." She looked longingly at the walls. "Built this place so that if they lost, they could regroup here…"

Shawn said quietly, "But they didn't come back, did they?"

"There are many lingering deaths in this world. To challenge the Wolf King is one of them. They were not the last Chosen to pass through, and over the years, this place became an outpost, a waystation for… *many*… that passed through."

Helesys and the others shared a look. She said, "On our travels, we've heard of other Chosen that failed, but we thought their numbers were few."

Beliah said, bitterly, "When one dies, they are reborn in another realm. But to seek the Wolf King necessitates finding a way to walk through worlds by force. There are many realms, so your words do not surprise me. But this realm, the bog, is the first step on the King's path—the very realms the king, himself, once strode. So all Chosen pass through here."

Shawn asked, "There's no other way?"

At that, a smile crossed Beliah's face. "No, foolish one. If you want to meet a King, you must go to them. If you want to meet God, you must seek the Wolf King—in his throne room. There is no other way."

"How many other realms?" Helesys asked.

"In truth, I don't know. Since coming here, I haven't left this realm." She left the rest unspoken. *And no others have returned.*

Beliah continued, "I don't remember how many years I've been here. The rest of those that stay in the realm slowly lose themselves to the bog. They become shells of what they once were. The men below know nothing but the hunt."

"We tried to talk to them," Shawn offered.

"I'm surprised they could talk," Beliah replied. She hesitated. "I had no intention of staying here, trapped, while everything I knew crumbled to ruin. I hoped the next Chosen I met might take my place." She waved dismissively. "Say nothing. I can see that you won't stay."

Taunauk asked, "What else can you tell us about the bog?"

"Follow the ruins. There is still some magic in the stone, and it has kept away the worst of the bog and its creatures. Past that lies the barrows and the rat-men. Show no mercy to them.

"And past that, nearest the seam, the cuckoo lies. Avoid it if you can. Run if you cannot."

Taunauk glared at Shawn, as if to silently chide him for his earlier remark about *strange creatures.* Shawn stared at the floor.

Though she nearly chuckled at her comrades, Helesys met Beliah's eyes and found a deadly seriousness there.

Beliah said, "There are many lingering deaths here, and not all of them are created equal."

"Oh, come on," Shawn said. "What does that mean?"

Beliah rose from her seat and shrugged. "We've lost many Chosen to that terrible creature. I'm not about to go near it."

~

Wearily, the heroes followed Beliah back down the stairs and outside. She led them along the ruins, following the remains of the crumbling structure as it led deeper into the bog. The world was quiet, and there was no trace of the hunters or of any other life in the mist or in the bramble above.

Following the length of the ruins, Helesys wondered if it might've been a tower long ago, stretching up into the sky before it fell.

They had walked in silence for some time, but Helesys felt compelled to ask, "What happened to the tower?"

"I am older than I look, but this place was ruins long before I came here." Beliah walked in front, and so Helesys didn't see her face, but there was melancholy in her voice. "This place is wrought with buried history. One need only look beneath their feet to find half-buried realms. The paths of the living paved by the dead and the forgotten."

Shawn said, "There are some cultures that say even the stars grow old and die."

"You are well traveled for one so young."

"...Something like that."

"Why did you stay here, instead of seeking the Wolf King?" Helesys asked.

Silence followed. Helesys didn't pry. She felt Taunauk and Shawn glance at her, but they said nothing.

Beliah slowed, but didn't turn. Finally, she said, "I was afraid. To see so many Chosen—so very many—like moths to a flame. How could I walk knowingly into death?"

Shawn shrugged. "That's all we've been doing."

"I suppose it is," Beliah replied.

"Better to shepherd them, then?" Helesys asked.

Beliah hung her head. She turned, looking wistfully off into the bog. "Better to live. This is where I leave you, Chosen. May you find that which you seek. May you succeed where all others have failed. And if not, may you find eternal rest."

Taunauk and Shawn nodded, then started to walk past her. But Helesys was overcome with an urge to speak.

"You were once Chosen, too," Helesys said. "You still are. Do not stay here. Do something. Do *anything* else." Then she walked past the old hunter before she could say something else.

Helesys, Taunauk, and Shawn walked into the mist and the gloom, following the ruins of the old world.

Helesys thought of the others that stayed in the Dungeon instead of seeking escape—instead of seeking the King. Before, she pitied them. Thought them weak—even when they stayed to protect others in their stead as Zhug or the Deacon.

Now, she thought of Beliah—*of those left behind*. An image came to Helesys, of the old hunter staying in the ruins while the rest of the Chosen passed through the realm or became mindless slaves to the bog. The image colored her prior journey like the sunset bleeding across the sky.

Even if the heroes escaped, the rest of the denizens were still trapped. Even victory and escape would ring hollow.

Helesys turned her attention to the fog, to whatever danger lay beyond, to the seam that lay deep in the realm. She walked in silence with her comrades, and buried her inner turmoil, leaving it behind as she strode past ruins of the old world.

~ ~ ~

The Barrows

Sometime later, the ruins sank beneath the muck, and the bog began to change. The trees had steadily grown larger, and were now three times the width of a Terran. Stranger, the trees had grown even closer together, forming a sheer wall of pale, twisting bark. Even the canopy above, once a mass of bramble, now resembled a cavern ceiling.

In the distance, the soft muck of the bog turned into murky water. The only way forward appeared to be through a number of catacombs—some of which were half-submerged.

They stopped at the edge of the ruins, a large stone block that lay like the end of a shoreline jetty.

Shawn put his hands on his hips as he surveyed their path. "Well, I'm not going in there." He pointed to the submerged tunnels. "No, thank you."

Taunauk grunted. "I agree. Better to stick to the upper passages."

"A cave by any other name," Shawn muttered.

"It could always be worse," Helesys said. Taunauk glanced sidelong at her. She added, "I know. *Don't give breath to fate.*"

Taunauk sighed and nodded toward the rogue. "That's *his* job."

Shawn feigned offense. "I'll have you know, I can usually go a realm or two without. It's only natural that Helesys should have a turn."

The three shared a laugh, and when the mirth died, Helesys cast *water walk* once again. Then they strode across the water to an upward sloping catacomb.

~

The catacombs stretched onwards and ever at a slight incline. For the most part, the passages were wide enough for the three of them to walk abreast. Helesys showed the way with her *warding light* and kept the light at her comrades' backs. The walls of the tunnels were smooth-bored, with only the slightest grain of bark— seeming almost made of white stone. The illusion was broken by the occasional bulbous knots of wood or thick trunk. Helesys thought back to the lost city, to the enormous cavern carved by the god serpent SHESLANG. These ghost-white caverns might have been bored by a similar creature, and the trees were trying to stitch the wounds back together.

For the first twists and turns of the passages, the heroes saw no other signs of life. If these tunnels had been made by something, it was long gone.

Helesys reached out her magic sense, feeling for the seam and any other lingering magic. She felt both things, and that they were growing nearer.

Helesys told Taunauk and Shawn this. "It feels like the seam is in the center of this place. We should find it if we follow the tunnels."

Shawn asked, "What *is* this place? Scratch that. I'm not sure I want to know."

Taunauk said, "You may find out sooner rather than later. Up ahead." Movement at the edge of the tunnel. Something scurried around the corner and down a connecting passage. Taunauk added, "Do you remember the buried hive?"

"All too well," Helesys replied. It was a dozen realms and half as many lives ago, yet she remembered.

Shawn asked, "So, uh, what happened in the hive? I wasn't there. Remember?"

The three stalked down the passage, and Helesys whispered, "There were passages, like this. It was all too easy to get surrounded or ambushed."

Taunauk added quietly, "It will be easier to keep watch with three sets of eyes."

"Yeah," Shawn replied, hiding his uneasiness. "Yeah, it will."

"What's the matter?" Helesys asked.

Shawn gestured at the walls with his white-bladed dagger. "All this. I don't like being underground."

"We're not underground," Taunauk muttered.

"You know what I mean.

They were twenty paces away from the connecting tunnel and the three of them fell to silence. Taunauk walked the last few paces and peered around the corner. Then he waved for them to follow.

Helesys peered around the corner and found blood splattered across the white bark. It was dry. Stained. There were faint streaks where a kill had been dragged into the gloom.

Shawn said, "Is it weird that I feel better now than when I thought we were alone?"

Taunauk sighed. "It changes little. We keep moving. Shawn, watch the rear. Helesys, watch the branching paths."

~

Taunauk led them deeper into the passages. Helesys walked in second, her gauntlet held high to light the way. Shawn followed, keeping his eyes on the passage behind them. Their path led slowly and steadily upward.

The smeared stains of blood grew more numerous, tainting the bottom of the passage like a dried riverbed. The smell of mud and earth was tinged with the metallic hint of blood. Occasionally, they would pass a connecting tunnel that descended; the smell of stagnant water and mold wafted from below.

Twice more, they passed connecting tunnels that led upward. The stains were thick, still glistening, still tacky, where death was fresh and not a memory. They paused at these tunnels, listening for danger, but heard nothing.

But they had never been lucky enough to cross a realm without danger—

And this was the King's Path.

They passed a bend in the tunnel and came upon a group of three creatures.

The things stared, eyes wide and unblinking in the harsh light. They were Terrans, or had been, and as the moment dragged on, Helesys saw all that was wrong with them. They were hunched over on all fours, naked, skin stained red. Their eyes were milky white, faces elongated into rat-like snouts. One of them crawled forward slowly, long nails clicking on the bark.

Taunauk whispered, "*Quietly*, Helesys."

Helesys kindled power. "*Restu sonmova, musremes.*"

~

The realm fell away and was replaced with the shared mind-space of the *holding* spell. The catacombs were unchanged, still lit by a semblance of the *warding light*, but now the edges of the light ended in thick mist. The three twisted Terrans peered out from the mist, half-hidden, before creeping slowly toward her.

In the depths, she heard the skittering of more of them. Dozens. Hundreds. And as she held the three creatures, she felt the attention of the horde drift through the tunnels, toward her.

"Damn," she muttered. So much for going undetected.

The three Terrans crept toward her on all fours, reminding her of rats.

Sharing mindspace with them, Helesys knew they had once been humans and elves. Once, they had even been hunters. Some of them might have been Chosen, just like Helesys. But they had stayed in the realm too long. Slowly, inexorably, the bog had eroded their minds, and then it had twisted their bodies.

Now, they were creatures of hunger and fear, and little else. Primordial and animalistic. Little more than made-things.

And as the moment stretched on, Helesys felt a pang of pity and kinship. In her death throes on the eternal battlefield, she had been much the same—her mind so shattered she felt little more than those basest of Terran emotions. It was only by the grace of elven technology and magic, and by the joining of her wand, that she grew to be anything else, that she lived at all.

For so long, Helesys had wondered why she could *hold* made-things and creatures beyond Terrans. Wondered why she was beyond so many other mages.

Some part of her had always known she was different. A truth she didn't want to see.

She watched the three rat men cut down. One was cleaved in two by an invisible axe, while blood sprayed from the necks of the other two. They crumpled to the ground.

~

The holding spell faded, and Helesys was once again in the real tunnels of the bog. Taunauk and Shawn stood over the slain rat-men—the barbarian scanning the tunnels while Shawn turned toward her.

Helesys stepped closer and said quickly, "There are more in the tunnels, and they sensed the spell. We don't have much time."

They jogged up the tunnels, moving as quickly and silently as they could. Chittering and scratching echoed through the gloom and grew into a cacophony. Soon, Helesys caught glimpses of other rat-men at the edge of her light as they funneled toward the heroes, pouring in through every tunnel.

They began to run through the tunnels, Helesys shouting directions to Taunauk as quickly as she could, lest they take a wrong turn. Helesys leveled her wand-arm, sending blasts of purple power into intersecting tunnels. She'd grown stronger as they'd journeyed through the realms—rat-men burst like sacks of flesh as the arcane power tore through their ranks.

In the harsh shadows of her *warding light*, Helesys saw nightmares. Some of the rat-men were vaguely Terran, but others were more grotesque—they lurched through the tunnels on gargoyle limbs, their mouths split with teeth so large they couldn't close. Others looked like hairless panthers.

Soon, the torrent of enemies reached their tunnel. But the heroes didn't stop. Taunauk cleaved through the rat-men two at a time, barely slowing as he ran. Helesys followed as close as she could, firing her gauntlet, leaping over bodies, and minding the backswing of Taunauk's axe. Shawn cackled behind them, hurtling over the dead and the still living; even with his arms still wrapped and powers suppressed, nothing could touch him. The heroes tore through the horde, plunging through the tunnels like a dagger through marrow.

But even the most powerful warrior can be beaten back by the storm.

From deep in the tunnel, a wall of flesh emerged—a rolling wave of rat-men that clambered over one another in a mad scramble. Helesys fired three blasts at the horde, but they didn't slow.

Taunauk roared, "This way!" He led them into a passage on their left. Helesys didn't protest—at least the tunnel was going steadily upward and not down to the flooded depths. Better to have the high ground than be trapped with the water at their backs.

The enemies were still numerous, but the heroes cleaved through them. Helesys channeled strength to her body, slamming the butt and point of her spear into those that slipped past Taunauk. Meanwhile, Shawn was a misty blur of speed—his wrappings half-undone. He leapt forward in blinks and flashes of movement, covering not just behind them, but leaping forward to thin the ranks around Helesys.

"We must go faster!" Shawn shouted.

The metal smell of gore hung heavy around them, and it was only then that Helesys glanced back to see the horde. Thirty feet away. As bodies slipped beneath the wave of flesh, singular rat-men stopped to feast; the creatures ate their dead and their wounded. Crazed with hunger.

Helesys turned and called upon her Ring of Winter. *"Murum glaciei tempestatemque!"* The tendril of frost slid through her veins and rushed out of her finger. Cold burst forth, spreading in an instant to cover the entire passageway. Helesys funneled more power from her gauntlet, bolstering the spell, thickening the ice. Moments later, the horde slammed into the wall—only faint shadows of rat-men shown beneath.

The heroes kept running and slaughtering their way upward through the thinning ranks. For now at least, the rest of the horde was held at bay by the ice.

When they reached the next connecting tunnel, Taunauk reeled—he raised Everfall, and a volley of arrows slammed into his shield. Six hunters sprinted toward them, bearing weapons and torches. Rat-men poured through the other tunnels.

The heroes ducked, and Helesys fired five blasts from her gauntlet. Two of the hunters were struck and bowled over. More arrows flew toward them, fired from the archer in the back of the group. They thudded against Taunauk's shield. One flew high overhead—

One struck Helesys in the right shoulder. She cursed and ducked low behind Taunauk, feeling the wound but finding only metal. The arrow had glanced harmlessly off the metal shoulder of her gauntlet.

"I'm fine," she muttered.

The only escape was down the tunnel to the right, but if they ran, the hunters would have a clear shot at their backs. The heroes were pinned down at the corner. Helesys dredged power from her gauntlet, then compounded it with the Gar of Shéslang. Her warding light dimmed, replaced with flashes of purple as power crackled around her gauntlet. Metal rattled in her shoulder. She readied a spreadblast powerful enough to cover the entire passageway.

She stood and met the eyes of the archer—before he could fire, she let loose. Power erupted from her metal hand, and purple flared, nearly blinding her. Instinctively, she braced her body with the power she could spare.

"Run!" Taunauk shouted, voice muffled by the ringing in her ears.

Helesys rekindled her *warding light* and followed in a mad dash. She spared only a moment to look toward the aftermath—

Two of the hunters were sprawled across the cavern, but four stood shakily, already rising and readying themselves for a chase. Helesys cursed—they were warded by powerful magic… and something else. She felt a stirring of the bog, as if the realm itself was bolstering the hunters—using them as weapons against the heroes.

~

The heroes sprinted through the white caverns, carving through rat-men and dodging arrows from behind them. Helesys twisted her metal arm behind her and fired errant blasts, but she didn't pause to see if any struck true—

They couldn't stop and they couldn't slow. For now, the caverns rumbled and they could hear the scratching of the horde. It was beneath them, Helesys was sure, and gaining on them. Their path had grown erratic to keep from being shot from behind, and with each turn, more rat-men descended on them.

She could block tunnels with ice, but Helesys was saving her Ring of Winter. Its magic was too valuable and versatile to waste, and there was no telling how much further they had to go, or how much longer they would need to fend off the creatures.

But as the heroes turned into another junction, arrows came from their left. They slammed harmlessly into Taunauk's shield, but vines erupted from the impacts. The green ropes lashed to their arms and legs, and then to the cavern walls, entangling them. Taunauk and Shawn were quick, already cutting themselves free, but they lost valuable time—too much time.

Rat-men leapt onto Taunauk's back, and toward Helesys and Shawn. Helesys twisted her metal hand and blasted the creature, and it fell lifelessly at her feet.

Six hunters rounded the tunnel behind them. More rat-men came from the passages above, and the floor beneath them trembled with the approach of the horde.

Helesys bolstered her strength and wrenched her arms free from the vines. Chest heaving, she called on her ring and turned toward the lower tunnels—toward the horde.

The trembling grew to a rumble.

Helesys grit her teeth. She was tired of running.

She dredged power, compounded it with the spear, and focused all her might. She reached out to the minds around her: The hunters were warded and not worth her effort, but the rat-men were simple creatures. Their simple, twisted minds would be hard for any other mage to hold, but not her.

The world fell away. The axe and blades of her comrades became blurs. Taunauk's roars and the screeches of the rat-men grew quiet.

Helesys reached for the minds of the horde. Her *warding light* dimmed, and at the very edges of the gloom, the uncountable horde slowed to a crawl.

In the mindspace, Helesys stood as a giant, and the rat-men as ants. Though they worked in unison, each creature cowered. And though they were slaves to the bog and the tunnels of the barrows, the bog was quiet in comparison to the voice of the giant.

"*Kill the hunters*," she commanded.

The horde advanced.

"Run!" Taunauk shouted. He grabbed Helesys by the arm and dragged her through the tunnels.

"Do not worry," she muttered, but her voice was faint. Helesys felt clammy and like she might fall to her knees and wretch. She felt hungry, desperate. Lost. Like a voice drowning in a sea of rat-men.

They rounded the corner of the junction and leapt out of the way of the approaching horde. Then Taunauk and Shawn slowed as they realized that the rat-men were no longer attacking them. They were running past.

The horde turned the other direction, barreling straight toward the hunters.

Helesys felt the horde tear into the Terrans. Dozens of the horrid creatures descended on the hunters. Bites and scratches came to her in a torrent of images like flashes of lightning. She winced and suppressed a wretch as the creatures ate them alive. Their flesh was warm.

Helesys stumbled and fell.

"Helesys, we have to go," Shawn said. His voice was urgent. Faint.

"Carry me," she muttered.

Taunauk cradled her in his arms and they were running a moment later, but it all felt so far away.

It wasn't enough, and Helesys was tired of running.

"Kill each other."

The rat-men obeyed. The horde turned on itself, and even the decrepit stragglers at the ends of the passageways descended on each other. She held the spell. Even as the light faded. Even as the screams and screeches grew deafening. Cut down like a field of wheat. Like blood drained from a bucket.

When the tunnels were quiet, barren, and slick with blood, Helesys passed out.

~

"She's waking up," Shawn said. Then louder, "It's okay. We're safe."

Helesys blinked, and the dim tunnel came into view. Taunauk and Shawn were beside her, the three of them were slumped against the wall of the tunnel. She winced at the pain in her skull. Helesys pushed herself back so she could sit all the way up. Her entire body was sore, and her metal arm burned as if it were smoldering in a fire.

"How long was I out?" she asked.

Taunauk replied, "An hour or so. Not long."

Shawn added, "You earned it."

A speckle of red coated Helesys's pants and boots. She looked to her comrades and saw they fared even worse. Both of them were coated in it.

"Can you walk?" Taunauk asked.

"I think so."

Shawn held up a hand. "I think we can spare a moment's respite."

Helesys relaxed. Twice now, Taunauk had carried her—something she'd sworn early on that she would never ask. The throbbing in her skull was already lessening, but she still felt like *stercus*. She wouldn't argue with a rest.

"Besides," Shawn said to her, "now that we have a minute, you can tell us about those visions you saw in the gallery."

Helesys forced a laugh, which came out pitifully. "You first. I lost you when we were flying—I mean, dreamsurfing. I didn't see you again until the factory."

Shawn said, "Well, not much happened. I surfed through a few dreams and then I fell. Became mortal. I don't really remember much about either; even in the gallery, the memories are kind of vague. Like waking up from a half-remembered dream. A mortal body can't contain all of it, can't understand all of it.

"I didn't really know what to do with myself at first, so I became a mercenary. Did stuff I wasn't proud of. Killed a few people… It's weird to think about, but when someone dies, they don't dream anymore. I took their dreams away. Became an antithesis to the god I was.

"I found the factory. The grandfather, Eugen, and his grandson, Galli. I'm pretty sure I already knew her from her dreams, but I don't remember—not for sure. Kids dream so much more than… Anyway, I made up my mind that day. I stayed. Figured I would rather toil away in the factory than do mercenary work. Spent the time I could with the old man and Galli. They were my anchor…

"Then you found me," Shawn said. "Thanks for that, by the way. Don't remember if I told you thanks. I might've been stuck there, otherwise."

Taunauk added, "We all might have."

Shawn chuckled uneasily. "Yeah… So, Helesys, did seeing your memories help at all?"

Helesys breathed slowly, trying to steady herself. She didn't know whether it was the recent exertion, or the revelation that weighed so heavily on her—

Who was she kidding?

"I was injured on the battlefield," she started. "Badly. Not just my body, but my brain. There wasn't much left of *me*." Helesys took another breath, and recounted the words of her wand. "I was dying. My higher brain functions were shutting down. I was nothing but pain, anguish… raw emotion. I didn't even have the ability to scream.

"This," Helesys said as she held out her gauntlet and flexed her metal fingers. "This isn't just a prosthetic. The wand inside is connected to my spine and my brain. The wand and I became one… but it took time.

"That was my revelation in the gallery. I'm a *made-thing*, like this spear or your shield, Taunauk."

Silence lingered, and when no one spoke, Helesys continued. "When I woke, I was angry. *So angry*. I think… Even then I knew what they'd done to me, what they'd made me into—even if I didn't have the words for it. That's why I left *Novissimé*. I was looking for *Sala Gehenna*—That's what my people call it: *The Dungeon*. I… I think I thought it could undo what happened to me. Somehow."

In spite of her anguish, Shawn was smiling. He said, "We were all looking for it. *That's why we were together*. Taunauk was looking for the lost souls of his people. You were looking for a way to remake yourself. I think I was looking for a way to ascend and become a wisp again. The elves knew about the Dungeon, so we sought them out… That's why we got trapped together."

Helesys glanced at Shawn. "Then why weren't you with us?"

"I'm with you sometimes," Shawn pointed out. He shrugged. "I don't know. It's still technically a theory."

Helesys nodded. "At least now we know." It helped, but it changed nothing.

Taunauk saw her, and said quietly, "You are not a weapon. You are Helesys of Great House Byyra, and you are my shield sister. My friend."

Helesys smiled and nodded quickly—eyes watering only a little. It didn't assuage her turmoil, but it was easier to bear with comrades. With friends.

Shawn put a hand on her shoulder. "Mine too." Then he turned to Taunauk, brow wrinkled.

Taunauk grunted. "You're a friend and a shieldbrother, too."

~ ~ ~

Cuckoo's Hollow

The heroes continued through the tunnels by Helesys's *warding light.* She had extended her senses and found little life remaining. The few rat-men that were left alive had retreated—moving as far away from the heroes as possible. Even though they were simple creatures, they seemed to know that Helesys had been responsible for their deaths.

So, they traveled in peace and silence through the gloom, at least for a time.

Helesys could already sense another presence—not the remnants of the rat-men or the vague ocean of roots that was the slumbering bog. No, this was something else entirely.

It felt like a dark hole in the realm, like a candle of darkness in her magical sight—shadow she couldn't penetrate. But she knew it was alive. She could feel it staring back at her, feel it shifting in anticipation, like a panther about to strike.

And the seam was past the void, maybe even inside it—it was impossible to tell. There was no going around it.

Helesys told Taunauk and Shawn all of this.

Shawn merely shrugged, and replied, "Another dark god or lingering death, it is. Maybe this one can talk. I'll work my godly wilds on it."

Taunauk added, "Yes. Maybe it will keep you and let us go—*wait*. The tunnels end." At the edge of the light, the tunnel opened wide. The heroes stalked forward slowly, and Helesys's *warding light* pushed aside the darkness.

The ghost white bark of the tunnels gave way to an enormous cavern, so wide, tall, and vast that her light found no walls—Helesys could only feel with her magical senses that they were enclosed. This was the void that she felt, and now that they were standing inside it, she thought it more closely resembled a gaping wound in the realm.

The air was deathly still, the ground beneath their feet turned spongy but bone dry. What might've been a thin layer of moss wasn't green but vibrant mixes of colors, like oil spilled atop water. Stranger still, in the corners of her vision, these colors on the ground shifted, but when Helesys looked directly at them, they ceased all movement. She reached out with her magical sense, dredging power to do so—pushing back the veil of darkness. Vibrant color receded from the ground, revealing ash and dirt—

Pain wracked her skull, and Helesys released her power. Oily color returned to the floor.

"Are you alright?" Taunauk asked.

Helesys nodded and wiped her brow. "Something powerful lurks here."

"Then we should not linger."

Shawn nodded. "I agree." He kicked idly at a swath of green pooling at his feet. It scattered like snow and pooled again like oil.

Taunauk led them deeper into the gloomy hollow. For some minutes, they saw nothing but darkness around them and psychedelic colors beneath their feet. The *nothingness* weighed on Helesys. Even though her prowess felt unaffected, her vision was limited and her magical sense was dulled. She would not abide this place any longer than necessary.

They came upon scattered boulders. They were mottled gray and brown. Most were half as tall as Helesys, but others dwarfed her—standing two or even three times her height.

Taunauk lingered at one boulder that stood his equal. It was cracked from top to bottom, as if a wedge had been driven through the top enough to see through the other side but not split the stone completely. The barbarian stared, his face twitching intensely.

Helesys put a hand on his shoulder. "Taunauk, what's wrong—"

"Look at it," he whispered, and turned away quickly.

Helesys and Shawn stared at it, and she felt growing pain in her skull. She sensed that the boulder, like the ground, was an illusion. She persevered.

Slowly, the image of stone receded, leaving a thin, greenish shell in its place. The crack was still there, revealing the inside. The bodies of several Terrans were slumped against the walls of the shell, twisted together, and half-decomposed. For only a moment, the smell hit her, sickly sweet and rotten. Illusion pushed aside, Helesys saw the ash pooled at the bottom of the egg—eggs filled with ash instead of yolk.

Helesys stepped back, the image of the egg morphing back into stone. Her stomach turned as her eyes looked again at the glistening rainbow that coated the floor.

Shawn reeled a moment later. "What in the name of—"

"You shouldn't stare." The heroes turned and found a Terran at the edge of the gloom. The human stood completely nude, coated in the oil—ash—that littered the realm.

"What are you?" Taunauk asked, axe and Everfall shield at the ready.

"This place is exactly as it should be," he said without looking. He walked toward them nonchalantly, hands clasped behind his back, as if he were surveying a park or a fine museum, pausing to stare at the boulders he passed. "You see exactly what you need to see. No bother looking deeper."

Helesys kindled power in her gauntlet. "Exactly what *you* want us to see."

"That's right." He was twenty feet away now. Close enough to see that his hair was matted and unkempt, that scars covered his body beneath the colorful oil.

"Are you the Cuckoo?" she asked.

"A hundred languages… a hundred names they've given me. I *hate* that one." He turned, eyes unblinking. "That is why I eat you."

Shawn chuckled nervously and pointed his dagger at the man. "You know, most times I wonder whether it's good sport to kill a man, or a creature, for that matter. But you, you creepy little shit, you I don't feel the slightest bit bad about."

"The feeling is mutual." The man's eyes rolled back in his head and Helesys felt something creeping in her skull. The psychic touch of the creature. It felt as if she'd stuck her hand in cold oil—

And it was gone just as quickly. Taunauk's skin glowed golden, and smoke wisped from Shawn's body. From the surprised looks on Taunauk and Shawn's faces, they'd felt it too.

The man's face wrinkled in confusion, and he pointed at each of them in turn. "A godling, a vessel of souls, and a mage—a made-thing. No wonder you've made it here…"

Without warning, the man ran forward. Before he could close the gap, Helesys raised her gauntlet and fired. Purple power surged forward, slammed into him, and knocked him backward. The man rolled across the ground, his torso nearly splitting in half as he came to a stop against a boulder. Colorful oil—ash—spilled out from inside him.

She stared in shock. She had spent so much time fighting monsters and horrors… Even though the dead thing was clearly not human, he still looked like it. It had been long since she'd killed a human or an elf.

Helesys looked away, off into the gloom. For a moment, she felt the void around her shudder—not the ground, or the air, but space and darkness.

"That isn't the end of it," Helesys said quietly. "Now it knows we're not to be trifled with."

"Good," Taunauk replied.

~

The heroes walked deeper and the illusory landscape stretched out endlessly. Cracked boulders and oil—shattered eggs and ash. Helesys knew what the illusions really were, and she could see through them if she chose, but each time pained her. It felt as if she was quicker to see through the false images, but the deeper into the Cuckoo's hollow they walked, the stronger the creature's influence grew; they were at an impasse.

Hunger made them weary, and they paused to rest in the middle of a clearing, sitting with backs to each other and weapons at the ready. They ate clutches of lichen and snowberries, though these were running low.

Shawn broke the silence. "So we're immune to the creature's power."

Taunauk replied, "It appears that way."

"But it's not just going to let us walk through here."

Helesys said, "That's doubtful. It might be amassing to attack us now for all we know."

"Perhaps," Taunauk grunted.

Shawn said, "You don't seem so sure."

"The strongest warrior is not always the most capable."

"You're going to have to explain that one, big guy."

Taunauk added, "The strongest warrior does not need to fight to prove themselves. They can win by intimidation. They are not as practiced. I guess that the Cuckoo's power is singular and overwhelming. Effective against all others, save us. Like a master swordsman whose only blade cannot cut their opponent."

Helesys finished her last bite and said, "It *will* come for us." Even then, she felt the shifting of the void. Agitation.

Taunauk replied, "Yes, like a hungry animal, and we will deny it with steel."

From the gloom came a voice. "You think too small."

An elven woman walked into the light. Slender and young, but coated in oily grime like the man before. Her face was twisted into a smile.

The heroes stood, and after a moment's hesitation, Helesys raised her gauntlet and fired. The blast struck the woman square. She crumpled and rolled back into the darkness.

"Glad that's settled," Shawn said.

Another voice came from behind them. "What do you hope to accomplish here?" They turned to see an old human woman walking toward them.

Helesys raised her metal hand again. "Passage to the seam. Sometime after that, the death of the Wolf King." She fired and broke the old woman.

A fishman walked into the light. "Neither can happen. Neither will happen." Its voice was raspy—Terran words forced through a strange throat.

Helesys fired. The impact hurled the fishman away.

"This is getting tiresome!" she called.

Another man. "I admit, your plight is curious. Most succumb readily to my power." Two more women behind him. Helesys fired a volley, cutting them all down.

Shawn muttered, "I don't like where this is heading."

Taunauk growled. "Be ready."

Helesys felt the veil of darkness stir, felt it bubble. From the shadows stepped a mass of Terrans—all nude and wearing the same blank expressions as the dead.

A man in the front spoke. "I offer you this once. Join me willingly, or—"

Helesys fired, and the blast careened through the man and through the crowd.

Another spoke without pause, "Or I will pull you apart."

"Are you really willing to lose all these hosts?" Helesys asked. "Seems a waste."

"I have more." The mob rushed them. Their steps rumbled like thunder, their faces twisted into silent screams.

Helesys dredged power, strengthening her body and her gauntlet. Behind her, Taunauk roared, and Shawn was silent as a ghost. The mob crashed into them. Helesys annihilated them with spreadblasts and broke two with every swing of her spear.

Behind her, gruesome sounds echoed—slices of flesh and crunching bone.

It was a massacre. Helesys and the others had fought monsters and gods… Once, these people might've been Chosen, but no more. Now the dead piled up around the heroes—nothing but naked, weak Terrans against their might.

When the last Terran was cut down, and silence fell, Helesys gagged. Quiet tears streamed down her face from the grisly act and from her twisting stomach.

"Tamir, forgive me," Shawn muttered. "They're… They're not disappearing."

Taunauk stared at the bodies, his face heavy and shoulders sagging. "It is a lingering death. A better fate than being left as they were."

Helesys breathed deep. Taunauk was right. It quelled her unease, but didn't absolve her.

~

The ground beneath their feet turned from spongy to gravelly, like they were walking across a riverbed. The stones still glistened with the oily, rainbow sheen.

For a moment, she pushed aside the illusion and saw the landscape for what it was: A plane of crushed eggshells and ash. Then the image of the riverbed returned. They passed other boulders—other egg shells, and Helesys regarded each wearily.

The deeper they walked into the Cuckoo's hollow, the larger the rocks became beneath their feet. The oil rose to a trickle, to a slow-moving tidal pool beneath their feet. *Ashen sludge*—the plague of the realm, and the ruin of a thousand souls.

"You, uh, still sure we're going the right way?" Shawn asked.

"Yes," she replied.

"You guys feel that, right?" Shawn asked. "Tell me you feel that."

The oppressing weight of the void was growing. Helesys had felt it since they first set foot in the hollow, but now it was enough that Taunauk and Shawn could feel it too.

Helesys asked, "Both of you saw inside the egg?" When they nodded, she added, "I used magic to push aside the illusion before, but both of you could do it as well. Endroggen blood magic and dream magic… and now you feel the Cuckoo's latent power."

She trailed off. The weight of the void grew, and at the edges of the light, they found a mound of rubble. Closer they walked, and the height extended up until they were looking at a mountain—one built on shells and ash. The flow of oil grew until thin streams formed, thickening higher up the slope.

Strange trees jutted out of the side and seemed to wave and shudder in nonexistent wind. Helesys stared and pushed the illusion aside—the trees were half-dead creatures. Terrans, giants, winged Terrans, lizards, and those too deformed or rotten that Helesys couldn't recognize them at all—if they were even of this world. The strange husks twisted their bodies and heads to stare at the heroes, but moved no closer; they were embedded in the mountain.

Pain wracked her skull and Helesys looked away, letting the illusion return.

"Where do we go?" Taunauk asked. "Up or around?"

Helesys extended her senses and felt the void shifting again. Felt enemies approaching. "There's no time. They're coming."

Rocks began to roll down the mountain, and in moments, pebbles turned into an avalanche. Stones and boulders the size of men followed. Many cracked and shattered as they fell, spilling rainbows of oil. The heroes ran to the far edge of the slope and waited for the worst to pass.

When the rockslide passed, a huge figure slid down the slope. It was a green-skinned giant, three times their height, skin stretched taut over sinewy muscle and bone. It slid to a halt and stood. Dozens more Terrans slid down the slope and came to a halt around the giant. Two of which were thin and grotesque—twin copies of the lanky creature, Pitiful Lull.

The giant bellowed, "Turn back or abandon hope. I will not allow you any further."

Helesys stepped forward. "We are going to the seam."

"Then go around my nest."

Helesys stared at the giant and dozens of eyes stared back. Taunauk turned suddenly—more Terrans had gathered behind them on the slope. The Cuckoo was amassing its army.

The weaver looked between crowds, then looked at her allies.

Shawn shrugged. "I'm all for going around." Taunauk merely stood stoically, eyes flitting between the groups.

Helesys's eyes fell to the grime covered Terrans—to the beings subjugated by the Cuckoo. Her and the others could avoid this fight… but should they? Should she leave these people to a fate worse than death?

Helesys stared at the giant, her eyes narrowing. "I killed a god once already." Only a handful of realms ago. Mr. Mask— the titan of blood and glass.

"*Helesys*…" Shawn whispered desperately. "We can't save them all."

"But we can save *them*," she replied. "*Restu sonmova, mendaxes!*" She flared power, compounding it with the Gar of Shéslang. Helesys's mind stretched, and the world fell away.

~

Helesys appeared in a foggy world. For a moment, it looked as if she were standing in a black sky. She took a careful step and found clear glass stretched out beneath her feet. Though she couldn't see the ends of it, she knew the glass extended to the limits of this place.

She shivered. This wasn't right. This mindscape should've vaguely resembled the rocky hollows.

Helesys spun around, extending her magical perception, trying to sense where she was and what had gone wrong.

A groan echoed in the fog above her. Helesys looked up and found a titanic white spear-point descending toward her, like a castle tower had been upended and turned into a javelin.

The weaver funneled what power she could spare to her body and leapt clear. She landed hard and rolled across the glass, just in time to see the spear-point crash into the glass. The tip shattered, a dozen feet of the thing scattering in pale shards across the glass. They skipped wildly with hollow chimes. A sweet smell lingered on the air like wine or honey.

Then the titanic spear retreated—vanishing into the clouds as quickly as it came.

Then Helesys felt the presence of another. She turned around to see a figure stepping out of the fog. A thin giant of a Terran, wearing deep blue robes and a white wolf mask. As Helesys craned her neck to look at him, her mouth fell agape—

She didn't know how, but the Wolf King had found her.

Helesys stepped back. So much of her power was focused on the Cuckoo, but she kindled everything left in her gauntlet and the magic spear. Even as power flowed through her veins and rattled in her shoulder, she felt like a child.

He stepped forward, arms folded in the sleeves of his robe. *"Helesys Byyra, you have come so very far across the realms…"*

As he spoke, Helesys shuddered. She'd heard his voice taunting her, resonating in her mind. But hearing it from behind the bone-white mask made breath catch in her throat.

"I offer you this choice, one time and one time, only. Join me or die."

When Helesys finally found her breath, her voice was only a whisper. "No."

The Wolf King chuckled quietly. *"What was that, child? Speak up."*

"Never," she said, forcing herself to stand taller. "We will defeat you and earn our freedom."

The King stared at her. The eyes of his mask were black voids. *"You would defy me… Maybe you will survive this path and make it to my throne room. It's been too long since someone has. But mark my words Helesys Byyra, you will die like the rest—on your knees."*

The words cut through her bolstered strength and seemed to chill her bones. It was everything Helesys could do to suppress a shiver.

"For now," he continued, *"leave the Cuckoo be. It is under my protection. Disobey me, and you will die where you stand."*

Her heart skipped a beat as the Wolf King spoke, and unconsciously she knew it was but a flick of his magic—he could strike her down right now if he chose. Taunauk and Shawn would have no idea what happened to her.

The Wolf King turned and started to walk back into the fog. He paused and said, *"Be careful, Helesys. Should you fall, your friends will surely die by my hand. What is a barbarian's strength or a godling's life against the power of a mage?"*

~

The fog around her and the glass beneath her feet disappeared and Helesys returned to the Cuckoo's hollow. The naked Terrans all wore looks of surprise.

Shawn asked, "Didn't work, did it?"

"Not like it usually does."

The Cuckoo's Terrans stepped forward from all sides, but were stopped a moment later by a voice that boomed through the hollows.

"The Chosen will pass peacefully around the mountain, and continue through the seam of this world. Let no party harm the other, or they shall pay the ultimate price." The Wolf King's voice shook Helesys's chest and rattled stones from the mound.

Shawn spun toward her, eyes wide. "Is that—"

"Yes," she replied, her eyes never leaving the Cuckoo's horde. Meanwhile, Taunauk stared into the darkness above, like he was hoping to catch a glimpse of the King, himself.

Hundreds of eyes stared at the heroes, and slowly, the Cuckoo's horde retreated into the darkness and up the mountain. Though it said nothing in protest, Helesys felt the void shuddering in frustration like a clenched fist, like a powerless child.

~

"So, what the *stercus* happened back there?" Shawn asked.

Taunauk added, "I'm keen to know, as well."

The three were walking around the mound of stones, giving the Cuckoo's minions a wide berth. Though they were hidden behind the shroud of darkness, Helesys felt them lurking. Watching.

Helesys recounted her experience on the plane of glass—what should've been a mindscape. How the Wolf King approached her and stopped her from harming the Cuckoo. "He said the Cuckoo is under his protection." She shook her head. "I don't understand it."

Shawn said, "Once you become a creepy, all-powerful overlord, I guess you find new hobbies."

Helesys stared off into the gloom. They'd traveled more than a dozen realms, met countless Terrans and wondrous gods… Yet for all they'd traveled and all they'd learned, Helesys still felt as if they wandered blindly. As if they only knew a fraction of the truth.

"Hey, uh… He's not all powerful, you know," Shawn said. "We'll beat him."

Helesys shook her head. He'd mistaken her look for worry. "It's not that. There is *so much* history here. Millennia of it. So much buried. So much lost to time. What if there are other secrets to defeating the King?"

Shawn shrugged. "We have the Ma—"

Taunauk's hand flew up and grasped Shawn's shoulder. "Not here. Do not speak of it."

Shawn nodded quickly. Helesys didn't know if he was more surprised by his near mistake or by Taunauk's speed.

They continued in silence, leaving the mountain of rocks—broken shells behind. There were other broken boulders—eggs, these too they left behind. They walked across a plain of oil that shimmered in Helesys's warding light.

Shawn spoke up, "Taunauk, not to dwell on bad news, but we still need to find the rest of your ancestors. How are we going to do that?"

Taunauk said, "My father can sense them. We are closer now than ever before. He hopes that they have coalesced along the King's Path, and that we'll find them in the next realm."

Shawn scoffed. "That's convenient."

Taunauk shrugged. "The lost souls do not wander blindly. They are Endroggen now, the same as they were in life, and they are drawn to spiritual places. The Godpeak and the River of Souls."

Helesys asked, "What if we cannot find them all before we escape?"

Taunauk sighed. "It is a possibility. To leave any souls behind is a failure." After Taunauk spoke, his eyes glowed with a fierce gold light, and he stopped walking. He stood still, staring out into the dark.

Helesys and Shawn looked at each other, then waited for their comrade, standing watch while he spoke with his ancestors.

Taunauk's eyes welled with quiet tears. Finally, the light faded, and the barbarian wiped his eyes.

"Are you alright?" she asked.

"Yes. My father thinks I'm too harsh on myself... He says that *any souls* saved counts as a worthy victory." Taunauk echoed his father's words, though he clearly didn't believe them. His massive shoulders were slumped forward, like a man who carried the weight of the heavens on his back.

"Your father is right," Helesys said. "Could any other Endroggen survive the realms of this place? Or carry the lost souls inside them? No one else can do what you've done."

Taunauk didn't meet her eyes. "You speak truth, as does my father, but nothing can change how I feel."

Shawn asked, "Isn't that what your blood magic is all about? Pushing things aside for later?"

Taunauk grunted in frustration. "It's not the same!" He stopped and stared down the both of them, fist clenched around his axe. "It is nothing to push aside pain, or rage, or happiness… It is the way of my people, and our magic comes as easy to me as breathing.

"But finding the souls of Accaelum? The day the dungeon appeared in the heavens was so catastrophic the elders saw it across time and space. I was raised to be a champion of my people, to be the vessel of lost souls. This is my purpose. It is why I was pushed so hard, denied so much. It is why I was born…"

Taunauk's eyes glowed golden—his father trying to speak with him—but he clamped his eyes shut, and screamed, *"ENOUGH!"*

He stood, chest heaving, and when he finally opened his eyes, the light was gone. "It is an easy thing to deny an emotion; I have done so my whole life. But I cannot push aside my purpose. What other reason do I have to live?

"I will find the lost souls of my ancestors—all of them," Taunauk said. "And then I will crush the Wolf King's throat in my hands. And when he is in his death throes, Shawn can strike the final blow as planned."

~ ~ ~

The Weeping Rent

The heroes pressed forward through the realm in silence. The glistening oil was all but gone, leaving solid rock beneath their feet. New roots and vines rose from the stone—different from the bone-white bark that made the barrows and the rest of the realm.

This new growth was deep blue and green, and shimmered in the light. It wasn't until Helesys knelt down close that she saw the truth: Quiet blue flames covered the bark—every inch of it. Helesys reached out her metal hand to feel it, and the flames flicked cooly between her fingers.

She marveled. "It's cold fire."

"It's covered," Taunauk said, and pointed to the vines with his axe.

Helesys dimmed her warding light, and the blue flames grew a little brighter, illuminating the dark like a dim candle. In the distance, the undergrowth looked like a twilight sea of blue.

"The vines are growing thicker," Taunauk added.

Helesys stood. "That's where the seam is. That's where we're going."

Shawn said, "I had a feeling you were going to say that."

The farther heroes walked, the thicker the vines grew, as if they were walking closer to the origin of them. Helesys held out her mundane hand to the fire, but felt no change in temperature—

The flames flicked toward her Ring of Winter, drawn to it. She moved her hand back and forth, and watched the flames change direction, but never growing closer.

Helesys found Shawn staring at her curiously. "Jealous?" she asked.

"Of your trinkets?" Shawn scoffed. "No. I already have everything I need." He patted his vest pocket, one of the places he could draw from his ethereal pouch. "I'm just surprised." He reached toward the vine, shaking his head in disbelief as the flames licked his hand. "*This* cold doesn't hurt at all."

She asked, "Did you ever find any daggers here in the dungeon, or did you already have all of them?"

Shawn smirked. "Kind of makes you wonder, doesn't it?"

Taunauk eyed his Everfall shield—one of the first boons they'd gained. Deep gashes marred the surface from their scuffle with the possessed wizard, Amadeus. Taunauk said, "It seems we didn't need much."

Helesys felt the mage-killer token embedded in her gauntlet. They'd gotten it and the shield from Zhug in their second realm. Now it was so familiar she barely felt the dull burn of its magic. It was as much a part of her as the metal arm and the wires laced into her flesh.

~

They walked in twilight with only the cold fire to light the way. Helesys kindled only the smallest warding light she could manage, if only so that it was easier to bring to bear, should she need it. It was almost imperceptible against the gloom.

The roots continued to grow, thickening to the width of a Terran, but never growing so dense that the heroes had to cleave through to continue. Helesys thought back to the beginning of the realm, remembering the twisting forest and the immense bark passageways of the barrows. The undergrowth here seemed stunted—almost normal—in comparison.

But they had not passed a single tree yet.

Helesys reached out with her magic sense. She followed the roots and cold fire out into the darkness. The roots coalesced around a single point in the distance. All part of a single root system. A single plant. And they didn't connect to the rest of the realm; the edges of the roots…

Helesys frowned. The roots near the Cuckoo's realm were wilted, diseased—the same feeling she'd had before about the Cuckoo. It was a blight upon the realm. But the other roots had been forcibly severed, the ends singed and scarred.

"You have that look about you," Taunauk said quietly. "What is it?"

She told both of them what she felt. "It feels as if this growth was cut off from the realm."

Shawn sighed. "This place keeps getting better and better."

"It doesn't feel like the Cuckoo…" Helesys trailed off. Perhaps Shawn was right. Perhaps both were diseases, quarantined from the rest of the realm. *Something* about the realm twisted the former Chosen into the rat-men. Could this grove have been the source of that foul magic?

Taunauk said, "I feel it too. It is not the same. And I trust your judgment." The barbarian glanced at her and nodded reassuringly.

Finally, they came upon a single tree. It rose from the stone like an obelisk, and rose to loom some hundred feet above them. The branches above were few—seemingly lacerated by the same blade that cut off the tree from the rest of the realm. The few branches and leaves that remained sagged like that of a willow tree. The whole of it was covered in cold, blue flames.

"Who goes there?" said a voice that shook the realm. The roots and the very stone rattled beneath their feet—originating from the burning tree.

"The Chosen," Helesys replied. "Spellweaver, warrior, and rogue."

Taunauk lowered his weapons. "Taunauk Aonar, Helesys Byyra, and Soldei Milent." For a moment, it looked like Shawn might correct him, but the rogue stayed silent.

"Chosen…" The word lingered heavy in the air. *"I would be happy if I were born a thousand times and never met your kind again."*

Helesys said, "You have never met us before."

"You're all the same."

Taunauk's eyes smoldered with golden light, but he blinked the power away. "I recognize the bitterness in your voice. A Chosen wronged you… What did they do to you?"

"You have the sight of an old one, so I shall tell you a story: You stand on hallowed ground. My birthplace—the birthplace of this realm. Before me, it was nothing but lifeless rock. The barrows, the swamp, the far reaches, are mine. This realm belongs to me.

"My roots connected this world to others before there were words for magic.

"I do not know how long passed, but Chosen came to me. They sought the death of the Wolf King. They passed along my roots like steady rain,

and gave no thought to the destruction left in their wake. Whole realms burned because of you… because of the Chosen. They sought an end to their suffering. Sought salvation. There is no salvation here."

When silence fell, Taunauk asked again, "What did the Chosen do to you?"

"The Chosen stayed in my realm. They built monuments to their folly. But it would not last. My very essence corrupted them. I was powerless to stop what they were becoming. Soon, they were so mindless they turned on their brethren.

"A Terran came to me. Blue skinned, bearing sword and armor made of glass. His breath and heart were cold and uncaring. He sought knowledge or magic to defeat the Wolf King. I had none to give. When he learned of the suffering of the other Chosen, he grew angry and cursed me.

"Cold fire burns eternal, never consuming, never dying. He cut my roots, severed me from my birthright. Blinded me. I will never heal so long as his curse remains. This is my answer."

"There is salvation," Helesys said quietly.

"The Wolf King still lives. There is no salvation."

Helesys replied, "We will see for ourselves. Will you let us pass?"

"I have a request."

Taunauk replied, "Name it."

"End my curse, or kill me. I have lost hope that the Chosen of ice and glass will return. He is likely dead—truly dead."

The heroes turned to each other, faces a mix of solemn and shocked. Shawn asked, "Can… Can we do that?"

Taunauk turned to Helesys, "Can *you* do that?"

Helesys looked over the burning tree. She'd negated magic before—done so effortlessly in the midst of battle. But as she looked upon the cold fire, she doubted.

She could feel the latent power in the cold fire. It did not pain her to touch it, but it was not meant for her. Were she to attempt to negate the spell, the curse would turn to her. Magic powerful enough to burn eternal was infinitely more danger-ous than a fleeting spell conjured in battle. Negating it would be that much harder.

In contrast, the tree's power was faint. Smothered. Dying.

It was an easy thing to grant death, but then the path they walked was not easy. If Helesys could negate the curse, prove herself greater than the mage that bestowed it, then perhaps they really would have a chance were so many other Chosen had failed.

"I will try," she said.

"Wait…" Shawn said. "Should we do that? What if the realm can rebuild?"

Helesys shook her head. "The only one left here is Beliah. The Chosen—the rat-men are dead. Perhaps it is better if the tree reclaims the realm. To kill it would just send it elsewhere."

Shawn's face soured. "We could leave it. Who says we have to change anything?"

The tree rumbled quietly. *"Should one suffer forever for their mis-givings?"*

"No, they should not." Taunauk said. He looked at Helesys expectantly. Shawn turned away.

Helesys reminded herself that though they journeyed to-gether, they would never agree on everything. And she would not leave the cold fire to burn eternal.

"Very well," she said.

Helesys reached out with her gauntlet, then paused. She looked to the Ring of Winter, and saw the blue flames were drawn to it. She switched the Gar of Shéslang to her metal hand. Then she reached out to the flames with her elven one. The flames coalesced around her hand, and the crystal ring be-gan to glow with a molten light.

Through the ring, she felt the curse, and through her gauntlet and her wand, she understood it. For a moment, she'd hoped that the ice-wielding Chosen had been the original bearer of the ring, but she knew now that was not the case. The curse did not originate from the ring, but it longed to end—to return to *something*. To *someone*.

Helesys smirked. Then she spoke in the old words:

"Vocote, frigus flama maledicum. Revertere adme!" I call you, curse of cold flames. Return to me!

The blue flames flared at her words and began to flow like icy water down the bark and across the roots toward her. It felt as pins and needles to the touch, and Helesys kindled strength as the flames crawled onto her hand. Up her arm. Not stopping.

In the upper branches of the realm, darkness grew as the curse receded.

Soon, her elven arm was hidden in blue fire, and still more came. As the world grew dark, Helesys was bathed in blue light.

Shards of ice grating across her skin as if they were alive, as if they were trying to plunge into her. She called on her wand and the magekiller token—on the Gar of Shéslang—until her body was numb from power.

Cold fire crawled up her neck, over her face. It consumed her.

She gasped as it covered her eyes and slipped down her throat, like she'd been plunged beneath an icy lake. Her chest spasmed, and no sound escaped her lips. She doubled over in agony, holding desperately to the spear to keep from falling.

Helesys saw nothing but shimmering blue light. Heard nothing except her dry, desperate gasps.

Blindly, Helesys reached out with her magic sense. The last remnants of curse were nearly upon her. The pain was nearly over. Only a few more moments.

It was not a simple thing to end a curse—worse to end a curse placed by another. So, Helesys tricked it. She was neither the curse's master, nor a willing host. When the fire was gone from the realm, and Helesys was ablaze with light and cold and pain, she called upon the Ring of Winter.

The fire dimmed just enough for Helesys to see the concern on Taunauk and Shawn's blue faces, but she held up a hand to stay them.

The Ring of Winter tugged at the fire, gently at first. But the curse *knew* this was not its master. So it refused. The ring pulled like it was dragging an unruly child. The curse screamed like a thousand sitar wires severed at once.

And as the fire struggled, the ring's power flared. It felt as if a wolf had pounced, and bit down on a foal, and was dragging the dying thing into the brush—

Cold fire sloshed over her body, simultaneously pulled toward the crystalline ring on her finger, and pulled beneath her skin toward the icy tendril that ran along her nerves.

Helesys's skin grew numb, while muscles ached, and her bones burned. Jolts of pain flooded her nerves, and she felt the icy reach of the tendril grow. The ring drank in the power of the curse, and the tendril slithered down her back, her legs, and even pried its way into the connections of her metal arm. Pain gave way to shivers of discomfort. Helesys had fallen to her knees, still clutching the spear for support. The pain receded enough for her to open her eyes. To gasp for breath.

Blue had all but faded from the world. The last of it smoldered around her elven hand. Around the ring.

Her first breaths were frosty. Her muscles and bones were cold, but they no longer pained her. They felt strong and deep as a frozen lake.

Soon, the curse was brought to heel. Even the cold faded, leaving only strength behind.

~

Helesys stood, her legs steady. She breathed deeply, but victory was short-lived.

She should be dead.

She was only spared by her artifacts of power, and by her wand—by intrinsically knowing how to wield and diffuse the curse. By being what she was.

Now, the curse lay dormant inside her. Though it had no mind of its own, it had a will—that of a weapon. The will to be used.

She would deal with it when she needed to.

Helesys was in the dark and kindled her *warding light*. Both Taunauk and Shawn looked at her with worry, but a smile crept across the barbarian's face.

Taunauk said proudly, "The very realm trembled."

Shawn grasped her shoulders, squeezing her arms, as if he were making sure she were still real. "Still solid. Still metal. Good."

Helesys gently pushed his hands away. "I'm alright, really," she said, forcing herself to stand a little taller. In truth, physically she felt fine, but she was deeply weary, as if she'd suffered many years toil in a single minute.

Helesys reached out to the ancient tree. "How about you, old one?"

For a long moment, the realm was silent, then the world began to groan. The deep tone echoes through bark, branches, and roots like a rolling wave. In her magic sight, Helesys felt the ancient tree begin to glow—felt it reach out with its own perception, like a waking giant.

The tree began to glisten. Red sap oozed from cracks and scars in the bark. Helesys relaxed her kindled light and found the darkness slowly filled by light from the sap, each drop glowing with a miniature sunset.

"I was damned by a Chosen one, and now I have been saved by another."

Silence fell like snow between them, and Helesys felt the slow measured breaths of the tree—if they could be called such a thing. Overwhelming relief. Even Taunauk and Shawn seemed to breathe easier in the aftermath.

The tree said, *"I know few words worthy of such a deed—my thanks and a blessing… The seasons pass eternal. May you linger in the sun of summer and spring, find beauty in the dappled fall, and kindle strength in the depths that winter brings.*

"I have fewer boons as reward. No spells. No metal, but… You who bear the ironwood shield, you walk with the spellweaver?"

Taunauk answered, "I walk with her as shieldbrother and friend." His words echoed as strongly as the god's.

"Then the boon I grant you shall serve all three. Set your scarred shield on my roots."

Taunauk held the shield, staring at the marred face of it, before setting it reverently on a thick root. The bark immediately around it twitched like a serpent, and red sap poured from the cracks. It crawled upward like ruby slugs and scabbed over the ironwood shield. Everfall glowed so bright it looked as if it had been set ablaze.

"Ironwoods are children of the Lapinatus, the Second Trees. The Lapinatus were my children." The light subsided, revealing Everfall. The shield was revitalized—unmarred—and now veins of red ran through the bark. *"No weapon made of Terran or mortal will ever scratch it, and none but the most ancient magics will harm its face. Your shield is as perfect as I can make it. It is the best boon that I can give you."*

Taunauk took the shield and looked upon it reverently before placing it on his back. "Thank you, elder."

From beside them, Shawn asked, "Will it hold up against the Wolf King? He will use all kinds of magic against us."

"Yes," the tree said, its voice lowering. *"He will call down the wrath of a god of gods against you, and you must answer."*

Helesys placed a hand on Shawn's shoulder. "We will succeed. We'll get you close enough to strike the final blow."

Shawn nodded, looking as if he was struggling to put on a brave face.

"Go. The King's Path waits."

Helesys reached out her magical sense. With the cold fire gone, she felt the seam—the air surrounding the ancient tree. The world was thin. She pulled and the realm gave way. Times before, she had felt many worlds at each seam, but now she felt one stronger than all the others. The next step of the King's Path.

A river that carved through time and space, laden with souls.

Helesys stepped through, and Taunauk and Shawn followed.

~ ~ ~

NEXT TIME ON
*A BATTLEAXE AND
A METAL ARM*
Book 17:

Hollow Solace
Available August 2022

Spoiler–Free excerpt from *BAMA 17*

As the fading monuments gave way, streams appeared in their stead, carving across the landscape—growing steadily deeper and more numerous toward the horizon. The trickle of water growing to a roar.

As they neared the first stream, Shawn stooped down. "Do you see this?" he asked, pointing to the surface.

Helesys knelt beside him. The surface of the stream appeared unmoving—not frozen. When water freezes, its surface turned smooth. This stream looked as if it had been cast in glass. It had all the ripples one would expect from water, but *it was not moving*. Stranger still, the stream sounded as if it were flowing.

Shawn pulled a coin from his pocket and tossed it into the stream. As it passed through the surface, the strange illusion was broken and the water resumed flowing as expected. This lasted only a moment before the coin vanished and the water turned eerily glass-like again. All the while, the sound of trickling water did not stop.

"Don't worry," Shawn said. "That wasn't my lucky coin."

Taunauk had been watching over their shoulders. "Is it wise to toss coins into a river of souls?"

"Oh, that's what that is?"

To be continued August 2022

Thank you for Reading

I hope you enjoyed reading this story as much as I enjoyed writing it.

If you did, I would massively appreciate a short review on Amazon or your favorite book website. Reviews are crucial for any author, and a starred review or even just a line or two can make a huge difference.

It's especially true for the start of a series. Thanks and I hope you enjoy the next one!

Looking for more Engrossing Fantasy?

You might like ***Tales from Another World,*** an ongoing short story series containing stories about sorcerers, druids, mortals, gods, thieves, and all other manner of Terrans.

The 2nd, 3rd, and 4th installments are out and they tie into the outside world of *A Battleaxe and a Metal Arm.* So, if you're looking for more engrossing fantasy stories, and if you want to know more about this fantasy universe, read on and see how deep the rabbit hole goes.

What questions do you have about *A Battleaxe and a Metal Arm*?

If you've read this far, hopefully you'll read a bit further—both in this book and across the series. I'm not sure how most authors write serials and how much of it is flying by the seat of their pants, but that's not how I do things. For all the major questions that might come up in BAMA, I already have answers for 95% of them. Same goes for the major plot points, twists and climaxes. That might sound boring to some, especially some of you other authors who enjoy variations of writing into the dark, but I think having a solid blueprint is paramount to writing a long series.

So, what questions do you have about the story? Here are a few:

1) ~~What is the dungeon?~~ It's a soul trap of overwhelming size and power. But where did it come from? Is it a force of nature or an ill-made weapon, or perhaps something else entirely? In the real world, it looks like a giant cloud with faces writhing just beneath the surface. Helesys speculates that the

reason no one remembers it is because it's so horrific their minds blot it out!

2) ~~Who was Helesys before she got trapped~~? We've learned that Helesys was both a soldier and was the oldest daughter of the elven Great House Byyra.

3) ~~Who was Taunauk before he got trapped~~? There was an omen of a blight in the Endroggen heaven, Accaelum. Taunauk is an Endroggen barbarian who was raised as a warrior and a vessel. His purpose was to one day free the trapped Endroggen souls from the Dungeon.

4) How well did they know each other beforehand?

5) How did Helesys get her metal arm? Likely through injury, amputation, and replacement. She was likely fighting in the Eternal War, the war of the Elves against the Shadowkind.

6) ~~Who is Shawn~~? He is a wisp from the plane of dreams. One who walks through the dreams of elves and humans, while being neither. He has lived as both a god and a mortal. His kind is on the run from the elder god, Nimicus.

7) Why does Shawn feel so familiar to Helesys and Taunauk? The group speculates that they were traveling together for unknown reasons. Shawn worries that they were tracking him. This could explain why Helesys and Taunauk are always reborn together, while Shawn was usually alone.

7) Who is the Wolf King and what sinister plans does he have for our heroes? How did he come to rule over the Dungeon? How does the Gatekeeper factor into all this?

8) Who is the mysterious voice encountered on the white sandy shores of Meridian? Why do they seek the death of the Wolf-King? ...And why did they choose the heroes? The Voice might be the Gatekeeper... but the truth is still unknown...

Did I miss any questions? Probably. Connect with me and other *BAMA* fans on social media and compare questions!

I've got plans. I've got answers. And I've got them on a drip-feed. Keep reading and expect to find out a little more to the mysteries with each installment. Hopefully, you're as excited about this series as I am.

Connect with the Author

If you want to stay up to date on the latest about Samuel's publishing news and blog, check out his website and consider signing up for his monthly newsletter.

www.SamuelFlemingBooks.com

Samuel can also be found on Reddit, Tiktok, and Facebook.

Samuel Fleming is a Science Fiction and Fantasy author.

He grew up in Maryland, spending most of his time swimming and writing. Swimming gave him a lot of time to daydream, so the two hobbies complemented each other well. Idle day dreams turned into stories, some of which stuck with him for years. These days he swims a little less and writes a lot more.

He loves a good story no matter the medium: Books, TV, video games, comics, tabletop RPG's, or podcasts–most of which he attempts to share with his wife and three kids, and occasionally on his blog.

www.ingramcontent.com/pod-product-compliance
Lightning Source LLC
Chambersburg PA
CBHW030649190726

48286CB00008B/2729